Golden Mountain

Treasures from the Past

by
Rex Rian

Golden Mountain and the books of the Golden Copper series are dedicated, with the utmost gratitude and love, to the Highest Power in the Universe. Without that inspiration, these books, and the principles taught in them, would not be possible.

Acknowledgments

Thank you to Camile Rigby for her assistance in the creation of this series. I could not have done it without her.

To Jackson Bylund for his insights and amazing talents in the formulation and editing of this book. It is greatly appreciated.

My appreciation also to Andrew Balls for his assistance in producing the covers.

Finally, thank you to my wife and family for their love and support over the past few years while I've been writing these books.

Preface

Many years ago I was introduced to the story of an amazing couple. They were born around 1900 and grew up during challenging times for their community and this country. They experienced the Roaring Twenties, the Great Depression, and World War II.

Through it all, they not only managed to survive, but to thrive and build a small empire of wealth and service. This was done with Divine assistance and a plant called Cupressus Genus, or the Cypress tree.

Their story of the Cypress crop was not only in making the best of hard times, but thriving; first in helping themselves, then in blessing the lives of others.

Also, as we learn and understand the patterns of history we can foresee the events of the present and future.

Even now as I write this, the Earth and its inhabitants stand at a crossroad. What we, as the human race, choose in the near future will determine the fate of the world for the next 300 years and beyond.

With everything that is and will be happening over the next few years, can you still thrive, prosper, and help those less fortunate? **What is your Cypress Crop?**

May you come away from reading this story more at peace with the world we live in and more empowered with the ability to make a difference in your own life and the lives of others.

\- Rex Rian

Golden Mountain

Chapter 1 –
Southwestern Colorado, USA, January 21, 2020 CE,
Time Strand 1

Caves. Cold. Water. Darkness. Screaming prayers to any higher beings that would hear them. A flood of memories circled like a whirlpool in Austin's mind as he sat up in bed. Mere weeks ago—one month to the day—he'd experienced the second greatest terror of his life. Taylor, the only woman he had ever or would ever love, had pleaded with him to leave her behind. Leave her to die alone in an Antarctic cavern. Every instinct in his body begged him to do as she said, but he couldn't. He stayed in the freezing water of that wretched place with her, giving her the precious fruit they'd been sent to find.

For all that, she'd nearly died anyway.

Despite the sheer terror of that dark day, Austin found himself able to dismiss those emotions. Low as he'd been, those feelings were not who he was, but rather a shade series of sensations, ephemeral and long past. Besides, he'd been to hell and back to rescue a soul from damnation. Literally. Perhaps he would have been more traumatized if the Antarctica expedition or his brief tour of the inferno had not worked out in the end. But both adventures yielded happy endings, victories for both Austin and for Taylor in particular. It was almost funny that Austin feared the unknown future far more than anything that he'd yet experienced.

Austin glanced at the clock on the nightstand. Just a few minutes short of 7:30. Sunlight had already begun to seep through the thin curtains, and a twitter of birdsong offered pleasant morning music. The simple bedroom lacked much furnishing beyond the bed, nightstand, and dresser, but Austin didn't need anything more when he had Taylor in his life. He heard the shower turn off in the nearby bathroom and knew he'd see her soon. He idly wondered if she really needed to shower in her new supernatural state, or if she did it out of habit.

Austin was a changed man. A few short years ago, he had been, to put it in a single word, a disaster. Flunking out of college. Playing video games until all hours of the night only to sleep into the afternoon, missing his classes and skipping assignments. Wasting his own money as well as his parents' on junk food and online gambling until his family cut him off financially. Here he was now, though, self-aware and humble enough to know that he had progress to make and a long journey of growth and improvement ahead, but content, though never complacent, in his progress. His debts were gone. He was independent. He had the tools, knowledge, and principles to live a fulfilling life, all thanks to the teachings of Nicholas and Vivian Ryan and their Institute. Even so, though, a shadow of self-doubt haunted him.

"Hey, handsome." Taylor stood in the entryway to the bathroom, a long white towel wrapped around her body, her dark, wavy hair still damp from the shower. It ran to her shoulder blades, so it would be some time before it dried. The bathroom lights framed her slim, feminine form in golden rays like wings. It was the perfect visual reminder that Taylor had long been Austin's angel. Always there for him. Always a helpmeet. Taylor had been present for the hardest things Austin had ever been through—the financial withdrawal of his parents, his temporary expulsion from the Institute where he so loved to learn, and each of their daring adventures across exotic terrains. She was there to comfort and guide him. And even when she'd had to leave him when he was his most foolish, a younger, more naïve time he remembered with sheepish chagrin, she'd come back. She always came back. Even from death itself.

"Are you just going to sit there and stare at me?" Taylor put a hand on her hip and rolled her eyes. "Hello? Anybody in there?"

Austin's hand twitched to the other, where he absently stroked the wedding band around his finger. Almost one month of wearing it and he still wasn't used to the happy sensation of the metal signifying his marriage to Taylor. The ceremony, held at the Institute and officiated by Marti, had been small by the luxuriant standard of the Ryans, but wonderful. Despite the few hours notice, everyone they cared about was there, and that was all that mattered.

"Sometimes it's hard to not just stare at you," Austin said, glad for the thousandth time that he could express the feelings he'd long had for Taylor openly.

"You're so beautiful." The next words he said still held wonder for him. "You're my wife."

Taylor sighed in affectionate exasperation. "Yes, I am. And you are my husband. And you only think I'm beautiful because I ate some special fruit that made me that way. Translated being and all that, remember?"

Austin shook his head. "I thought you were the most beautiful thing I ever saw the moment I laid eyes on you, when you first came to tutor me in college." He rose from the bed and exchanged a long and loving kiss with his wife.

After Austin gave Taylor the precious fruit in the darkness of the Antarctic caves to save her life, she'd begun to change. Her chakras had cleansed themselves, sending her into a week-long physical and emotional tailspin of epic highs and devastating lows. She'd become truly immortal before she knew it, fast-tracked in her spiritual growth to an Ascendant Being. Austin didn't know what differences he'd been expecting, but their kisses were the same. In the best way.

The phone on the nightstand buzzed. A brief look at the bright screen showed Austin an email notification.

"Another job offer," Austin said.

"That's wonderful!" Taylor's beaming smile faded when she noticed Austin's lack of enthusiasm. "What's wrong?"

Austin's training at the Institute prepared him for emotional vulnerability. He felt no fear or shame sharing his concerns with his wife.

"I'm…scared," he confided.

"What on earth is there to be afraid of, sweetheart?" Taylor asked.

"Nothing, I think," said Austin with a self-deprecating smile. "It's just…we've been attending the Institute for so long now. And don't get me wrong, it's been wonderful. The best thing that ever happened to me. Aside from you, of course. But we've been sheltered here. Protected. The world outside is different. We won't be surrounded by friends. No Joseph or Maleena. No Marti or Geri or Talia, no…"

"No Nicholas and Vivian," Taylor said, understanding crossing her face. They both sat down on the bed together. Austin rested his head on his wife's shoulder.

"They've all been so good to us," Austin continued, "but we won't have them out there. And I'm not used to that anymore. I'm afraid I won't have a purpose out there, or that I'll…I don't know, get lost. Revert to my old self without Nicholas there to help me."

Taylor only nodded, understanding that her husband needed this emotional release.

"And it's so bleak out there right now. There's so much wrong with the world. What if there aren't opportunities? Not just for me, but for anyone?"

Taylor wrapped Austin in a hug, and he allowed her comfort to warm him, body, soul, and spirit. In some ways, he envied the added reassurance and confidence Taylor had gained since gaining Ascendancy. Immortal, infinitely wise, and infinitely beautiful, she could distance herself from fear in a way that he could not. Even so, Austin had made a choice to be with her, and he didn't regret it.

Nicholas and Vivian had told them about some options concerning Taylor's translated state. For seven days after she ate the fruit, she had the option to copy the effects of her Ascendant existence to another. She could have given eternal life itself to Austin. And he was sure she would have if he had asked. But the prospect of forever had frightened him, frightened him almost as much as Nicholas's suggestion that he and Taylor would become one mind and one heart in their shared immortality. So husband and wife had mutually agreed that it was for the best that Taylor be the sole keeper of her immortality. She would endure, while Austin would pursue Ascension on a mortal path, like the Ryans.

"Whatever the world decides to throw at us, we'll deal with it together," Taylor said. "We're a team now."

Austin laughed. "We've always been a bit of a team."

"Now more than ever."

Reassurance coursed through Austin's body at her words. With Taylor at his side, the dangers and destructions of the world would pass over them. Taylor's wisdom had developed at an exponential rate since she'd Ascended. If he didn't love her so, he'd be jealous. He sometimes had to be patient. It could be difficult to be infinitely more imperfect than your flawless wife.

Taylor changed into fresh clothes and bade Austin a quick goodbye. She was leaving for the weekend for a short visit to her grandmother and her brother a few hours away. It would be the first time she'd seen them since the wedding. Austin was staying to pack the rest of their things for their departure from the Institute. He'd pick her up and they'd start their journey together.

Taylor's visit wasn't just for her, though. She was taking Maleena to meet the family, too. Maleena, the sister that Taylor didn't know she had until recently. Although she was a new part of their lives, the long lost sister had found her place at the Institute and in Taylor's family.

The thought of Taylor's family growing and expanding drew Austin's mind to the fact that his own family was destined to remain forever as it was. While he didn't resent this fact, it still saddened him when he thought about it. Starting a family had been a part of his life plan for as long as he could remember. But with Taylor Ascendant, she was no longer able to get pregnant. It relieved some of the pressure from their marital intimacy, but Austin knew he wanted children somewhere down the line. And Taylor knew that, too. Who knew? Maybe they could adopt.

Overwhelmed and abruptly tired again, Austin decided there was no harm in getting an extra hour of sleep. It was a Saturday, after all. And once he'd done his morning routine, his plans only included the last bit of packing, which wouldn't take long. Then the long list of goodbyes would begin.

The softness and warmth of the bed lulled him back to a quick, if shallow sleep, the sort where he was aware of the room around him, a doze in which he still heard the birds calling outside and heard the rushed steps of Institute students leaving their rooms outside the door.

This awareness made it all the stranger when Tommy Campbell appeared to walk through the wall and into the bedroom.

Austin had met Thomas, or Tommy, as his friends knew him, shortly after visiting a grave site with the man's name marked on it. But Tommy wasn't dead. He and his wife Elsie had faked their deaths and attained Ascendancy themselves. Although

Tommy was really around one hundred and twenty years old, having been born at the turn of the twentieth century, his immortal body had restored him to his youth so that he appeared to be around Austin's age. His tanned skin still reflected a life in the outdoors, though the hard lines of labor had left the palms of his hands in his purification. He wore a gold ring, one that Austin knew matched a similar band that Elsie had, too. His dark eyes peered out from a youthful face, but they reflected wisdom beyond Austin's reckoning, betraying Tommy's true age to those who paid attention.

"Hello, Master Campbell." Austin asked, rising from the bed. "Am I dreaming?"

Tommy let loose a mischievous smile. "Sure, we can call it that." He had a great voice, powerful like a trumpet. But peaceful, too. "It would, however, be more accurate to say that you are in duality, or at the very least a form of it."

As Austin understood the man's words, he turned to find his own sleeping form still asleep in bed. He blinked, and something in the universe shifted. While Austin could still see everything in the bedroom in which he and Tommy stood, his vision expanded well beyond those frail confines. A vast and infinite dimension overlaid the earthly realm, a cosmic glory that hid beneath the mundane nature of perceived reality.

"Is this real, or just my imagination?" Austin said.

"Oh, you're not imagining anything right now, no. What you see now is more real than the three-dimensional hologram that mortals call the real world. The reality you think you know is an illusion. All before you now is true reality."

Austin nodded his understanding, having gone with Nicholas in brief forays into the realms of the infinite. He realized that he wasn't listening to verbal words from Tommy so much as he was watching the Ascendant man's very thoughts. This method of communication, purer and more beautiful than rough syllables from earthen tongues, conveyed clearer understanding and purpose than spoken words could ever hope to convey. Indeed, Tommy could see Austin's understanding with a clarity of vision greater than two people looking at one another.

As he took in his surroundings, Austin's thoughts turned to his wife. "Taylor's not here, too, is she?"

Tommy smiled, knowing what it was like to have such a wonderful life companion. "Yes and no. Taylor is here sometimes, though in other dimensions, as well. She learns outside the bounds of time and space. That's why she seems to progress increasingly faster than you do now."

Austin didn't bother to hide his frustration at the idea, letting the thought manifest in his consciousness for Tommy to see. "I worry that she's progressing without me. What if she moves so far ahead that she can't even relate to me anymore? What if she doesn't want me? Or what if her spiritual frequency is too high for her to be around someone like me?"

Tommy nodded. "I know. Taylor knows how you feel. And she knows your fears and insecurities. That's part of why I am here, to give you a gift. I'm here to teach you."

"Okay. What are you going to teach me?"

"Many things," Tommy said, that mischievous—though not unkind—smile returning. "I will show you the past and the present. And the future."

The Austin of only a few years ago would have chafed at such vague answers. Even now, as far along in his journey as he was, he yearned to ask Tommy to simply skip ahead to the part about the future. That was where his true concerns lay. But he had worked alongside people like Tommy and Nicholas long enough to accept the cryptic answer and let the lesson unfold to him as it went. In fact, Nicholas had taught Austin many of the principles he now utilized by telling Tommy's life story to him. Sometimes the truest and most profound learning meant taking things slow.

"I think I get it," Austin said. "This is like *A Christmas Carol*. Are you my Ghost of Christmas Past?"

Tommy laughed. "In a way, I suppose I am. For better or worse, though, I'll also be taking the roles of Present and potential Futures as well. But the comparison ends right there. You see, I'm not here to warn you about your chains or help you enjoy Christmas."

"What brings you to me?"

"I'm not a ghost here to save you from damnation." Tommy chuckled. "Heck, I'm not a ghost at all. In some ways, what I'll show you isn't even about you. It's about the world. If all goes well, you'll have a clearer understanding of its workings. You'll be able to see the future by examining things that were and are. In so doing, you'll be able to see Taylor and her mission with a better perspective. By extension, you'll know your own purpose, too."

"What is my purpose?" Austin asked. "Outside of the general path of Ascendance, I mean."

"That's not something I can plainly tell you," Tommy answered. "But know this: Ascension on its own is not purpose enough. There is no purpose—not one that matters, anyway—without others, without people. Your reason for being must be outside of yourself. It has to include others.”

“That’s what Nicholas told us,” Austin said, remembering his teacher’s words when Taylor first learned she had Ascended a month ago. “We’re to serve, share, and teach. And in doing so, bless others.”

“Correct. And each of us has an even more specific purpose beyond that, and it’s our duty to discover it and to do it. Do you remember Azaac?”

Austin did. Azaac, the man older than the United States of America, the sage with the face of a child between sixteen and eighteen years, but the unleavened wisdom of the ancients. He’d been little more than a cabin boy when he, like Taylor, ate of the fruit of life, found tucked away in a trunk of the ship on which he served. He’d eaten it out of desperation after the ship capsized in a storm, killing everyone onboard except him. Azaac had then spent months floating helplessly in the ocean, and then decades on a small deserted island, unable to die, but not really living, either.

"He was alone for so long, longer than anyone, Ascendant or otherwise, should ever be. He learned that he couldn't die, but had no purpose in living. How could he? There was nobody else around him. He had to learn to watch his thoughts and feelings or risk losing the Ascendancy he had so suddenly and unknowingly gained. Too much longer without purpose and he would have fallen into darkness. All because each of us need purpose beyond self. Helping others. Serving and blessing, like you said. Sorrow is often born out of a lack of purpose.

"And understand that this is about purely helping people. It's about cultivating powerful and meaningful relationships. No codependency. Just truly, honestly helping people." Tommy regarded

Austin with a mixture of abject joy and terrible sadness. "You have so much to do, Austin. I'm trying to help *you*."

"Help me what?"

"I'm trying to help you find your purpose. And make sure you're prepared for what is to come."

Chapter 2 -

The bedroom faded away around them, until all Austin saw was the seemingly endless expanse of the void called space. He felt like he was standing on solid ground but looked down to see nothing supporting him. Aware as he was of the nature of duality, though, this neither bothered nor puzzled him.

"When Taylor partook of that fruit, Austin, something remarkable happened." Tommy said, not commenting on the sudden change in scenery. "Are you ready to know it?"

"I hope so?"

Tommy smiled, appreciating the humility. With a wave of the Ascendant man's hand, a gleaming red thread floated before him. "This is time presented in its linear fashion. It is time as you and the rest of the mortal world perceive it to be. Taylor's choice has created several strands of time, a few different possibilities not only for how her life will proceed, but also how the world as a whole will move forward."

Austin took this information in without doubt, shocking and strange to him though it was. "How many strands are there?"

"Three." But Tommy hesitated. "There's a fourth strand with an extremely low probability of even occurring. For all intents and purposes, though, there are three." With a flick of Tommy's hand, three clear offshoots of crimson spread out from the central thread. A fourth one, gold in color, but faint and less vibrant, flickered off into its own direction.

Austin thought for a moment. "Which strand of time are we in right now?"

"Good question. This is the first one, in which Taylor chose to remain immortal without directly sharing its effects with anyone, including you."

"But when the other time strands happen, won't I forget this entire conversation? If Taylor changes her choice, won't that cause a domino effect that ripples through her every interaction, changing everything?"

"Yes," Tommy said matter-of-factly. He snapped his fingers, but nothing happened. "But look. These strands will not change or entirely cease to be, though one will be the final answer in a linear, mortal sense of time. You may not remember this conversation if and when the second, third, or even that distant fourth time strand happen. At least, you won't remember them within those pockets of mortal reality. However, your higher, more spiritual self will keep it all, and learn from it all. Even now, we are talking together because Taylor's higher self wants you to see and understand the world as it is."

"You mean, like a Taylor from the future?"

"In a sense, yes," Tommy answered. The threads of time disappeared as his attention went elsewhere. "There's a higher you further down the road, too. Taylor saw it. She saw your Fully Ascended self. But there are lessons to be learned before that can be."

Austin remembered Taylor's sacred experience at the tree hidden away in the watery caverns of Antarctica. He'd been aware that she was having a sacred experience, but not one so profound as all that. He marveled.

"You're afraid of the future, Austin." Tommy did not phrase his words as a question.

"Yes."

"That's not completely unwise, especially given your sphere of knowledge. But I'm here to take you into the past. I hope that what I show you can provide some degree of comfort."

Austin didn't have a clue how knowing the past could help him feel any sort of reassurance about the future, but he was more than open to letting Tommy lead him on. He spread his hands outward and open to the Ascendant man, offering all that he was to him.

"Take me wherever you need to," he said, "and I will do my best to listen and to learn."

Tommy smiled, all mischief gone, replaced with love and gratitude. "I know."

The pair suddenly appeared hovering above the planet Earth. But it was a far greener one than Austin had seen in pictures in science classes.

"I'm going to take you through different events through the last century or so," Tommy explained, "starting around 1910 onward. Much of it will have to do with my personal life and how it impacted both me and my family."

"What will that have to do with the future?" Austin asked. The question was not impertinent in the least. He was used to lessons made clear through storytelling. He simply wanted an answer.

"Greater calamities and cataclysms are coming to the world, Austin," Tommy said. Even as he said it, Austin remembered a similar warning from Nicholas a month ago. "And history works in cycles, repeating through the ages. Turmoil takes place in numbers divisible by seven. Every three-and-a-half years, every seven, forty-nine, and so forth. For you in the United States, it goes back as far as the Revolutionary War and further, beyond even 1678."

"Just the US?"

"No. This cycle is not unique to any single culture. It is a part of the collective human nature, going back eons, before history was recorded.

"But the US serves as a good example for our purposes. Just think. In 1994, the US economy took a tumble, including the worst bond market in over six decades. Seven years later, the modern world changed under the guise of 9/11. The Great Recession of 2008 followed thereafter, and so on.

"Elsie and I were both born in the year 1900," Tommy continued. "We bore witness to the tumult and tribulation of the twentieth century. When I was a child, men began to fly airplanes. Before I was seventy—but after I faked my death—astronauts went into space."

"That's amazing," Austin said. "I'd never thought of it that way. So much has changed. What was it like?"

Tommy smiled. "I will show you. And it's only changed exponentially since then. Technology that was thought of as science fiction in the 1950s and 60s make up your reality today. Smartphones, face-to-face communication over long distances, social media. But let me be clear about one thing."

"What's that?" Austin asked when Tommy paused.

Tommy raised a stern finger. "This much you need to know: the image of the world's face may change—technology is invented, lifestyles and fashions and social mores change—but the historical cycle always remains the same."

"How can that be?" Asked Austin, not doubting, but curious. "If our lives are so different, why are the cycles of history the same?"

"Because human nature does not change," Tommy answered without hesitation, "even if the world around humanity does."

"I guess we really don't," Austin said, thinking about it.

"No," Tommy said, his eyes on the greener Earth beneath them. "In a lot of ways, Elsie and I were lucky. We were able to almost continuously Ascend. We did it without even knowing it for a long time. I'm very grateful for the good start we had. It put us in a position to help others. It's far easier to serve and help other people when you yourself have already been helped."

Austin nodded understanding. He envied the seemingly young world beneath them.

"You're coming upon a special time, Austin," Tommy said, drawing the young man's attention away from the planet. "The world of humans moves in seven-year cycles and resets. The Jewish culture knows of this pattern. They call them Shmitas. For the US, this cycle goes back to 1776 and even to 1678. From our present day to 1678 makes for almost forty-nine sets of seven, or seven times seven, incredibly significant numbers. That makes *anno domini* 2022 a Jubilee of Jubilees for the land of America.

"There have been fifteen cycles of seven in the past century and change, between 1917 and 2022. The events of 1917 to 1945 make up twenty-eight years, or four cycles of seven. Events then mirror those of 1994 to two years from now, in the year 2022."

"And even though the times are different," Austin said, "the cycles reflect many of the same issues and calamities?"

"Precisely. All issues, both then and now, revolve around the Three Great Lies. First, and the least of these lies, is that money is bad, the root of all the evil in the world. Money is not inherently evil. It is just a thing, another form of energy, and the intention behind it can be for good or for ill.

"Second, that sex is evil, carnal, sensual, and devilish, and that women are the cause of that carnality due to original sin. Also, that women and femininity are weak and therefore lesser than men and masculinity, nothing more than the property of men. The truth to this lie is the polar opposite; sex is beautiful, edifying. Within it is found the very power of creation itself. Womanhood and femininity are equal in strength, existing in a balance with masculinity.

"Lastly–and this is the greatest lie of all, and most important for you to understand in what I am trying to convey to you–that humans are separated from God and themselves. This lie encourages the terrible deception that we must work to earn the love and acceptance of a formless, egotistical deity in order to obtain something we feel that we have lost. The belief that a god only loves certain favored groups of individuals, while others are damned to burn in hellfire because they are not part of that group. This lie is the root cause of almost all the atrocities in the world, having to do with the formation of groupism—the pitting of one group or individual against another because they are different, all the while fostering the belief that one group or another has a monopoly on the love and favor of God.

"The truth in opposition to this lie is that the Highest Power loves all creations without condition, and we are not separate from Source. We just believe the narrative that we are. When people think they are separate from the Source, they can feel justified in harming others, not realizing that they are hurting themselves in the process.

"But we're getting ahead of ourselves. We have other places to be." He snapped his fingers.

Chapter 3 -

Austin blinked and found himself swept away to another land and another time. And it was a grim scene. A brown and muddy wasteland sprawled before him, dotted with barbed wire, the remnants of shattered trees, massive craters, and the dead bodies of men and horses. Two trenches flanked the cragged and rotted land, each of them filled to the brim with soldiers. Austin was familiar enough with such visuals from the movies. Tommy had taken him to the site of a battle during the First World War. Although they observed from too far away for Austin to know which side was which, he could sense the emotions of the soldiers in each trench, all approximately the same—a cocktail of exhaustion coupled with extreme boredom and extreme terror.

"The Battle of Argonne Forest is about to start," Tommy said. "September 26, 1918. The offensive would rage for forty-seven days, leading

into the end of the war with the Armistice on
November 6.”

Austin nodded, taking in the awful sight, the
saddening sounds, and the putrid stench of the no-
man’s-land. What had this place been like before the
war machine arrived? What fair forests grew here and
thrived?

“Can you imagine the pain, Austin? These
men—many of them mere boys—once believed they
were about to enter a glorious adventure. They didn’t
have books like *All Quiet on the Western Front* or
movies like *Saving Private Ryan* to prepare them for
the horrors of war. They all thought they were off on a
grand undertaking. They thought they’d be home
before Christmas.” Tommy sighed. “But the Great
War would rage on for almost four full years. So
many lives lost, and for what? The First World War
was a uniquely significant waste of life. There were
no heroes or villains. Only sides. Separation. Each

determined to kill each other for reasons infinitely less defined than the endless web of treaties and alliances that carried the war to its massive scale.”

“But you didn’t fight in the war, right?” Austin asked. While he’d heard Tommy’s life story before, it had been a few years, and the details had become fuzzy.

“I didn’t, and I’m lucky for it,” Tommy said. “I was too young to take part in the conflict. The US entered the war later than the nations of Europe, not until April 6 of 1917. By the time I came of age, the Armistice was declared on November 11, 1918. November 11 is a significant day, remember that. The Armistice came soon enough to perhaps save my life, but it cost me friends. It cost the families of my little town. I remember their names to this day.”

Although Tommy did not vocalize the thoughts, Austin could still see the names radiating from his being. Dean Masterson, Miles Bertrum and others. Even now, over a hundred years later, Tommy still radiated profound grief for the losses. Indeed, perhaps his sorrow had grown even greater with the passage of time, his actualized being granting him even greater wisdom and insight into the suffering perpetrated by war.

"Just think how a war as terrible as this can change history forever, Austin. Men fell into insanity in the cruelly alternating boredom and violence of the trenches. They lost their feet, their heads, their minds. Countless lives were snuffed out, and those who survived were traumatized, but lived in a world that didn't have words beyond 'shellshock' or 'cowardice' to describe their psychological torments. The survivors were dubbed the Lost Generation."

Austin surveyed the grim scene before them. Hollywood screens had shown him wartime carnage, but he understood then that such imagery was almost always little more than a glittering imitation of a bloody truth. Such movies could at best demonstrate the horror of war (and at worst glorify it), but they could not prepare anyone for the true horror, tragedy, and humanity of such a vicious and efficient waste of lives.

"How did they go on?" Austin said. He knew he couldn't ever truly empathize with what these soldiers went through, but he'd gained an inkling of greater understanding by bearing witness. "How do you move on from something like that?"

"Some people don't," Tommy said, voice laced with sorrow. "Some people can't. It's too much. It's too awful. For those who do, though, it's a difficult journey, a painful reckoning with atrocities and visions that fortunately, you and I never had to deal with. Part of it, though, is found in the little joys of life, in moments that remind us that humanity still deserves to exist."

The scene shifted. Austin's awareness traveled through time once more to the winter of 1914, five months into the war. The no-man's-land between the trenches was filled with men, soldiers from both sides mingling together. They sang Christmas carols, bartered for cigarettes, exchanged prisoners of war. Some even played a game of soccer together. It was a striking picture, the pocket of holiday cheer amid the glum squalor of wartime France. Christmas celebrated between two trenches, acknowledged amid the barbed wire, mud, and blood of yesterday's violence. For the first time in months, the artillery fell silent, no longer raining shells on either side of the dreaded conflict.

"For a speck of time, the belief of separateness paused. And in less than a grain of sand through the hourglass," Tommy said, "the war ended. Enemy lines faded, nationalistic allegiances ceased to be, and soldiers could be the boys they each were at heart. Killers no more, they celebrated Christmas together."

"Why are you showing me this?"

"Oh, this Christmas Truce is appearing now as much for me as it is for you," Tommy said. "It's a helpful reminder that not everything is doom and gloom."

The peace of that short time could not last, though. Even as Austin and Tommy observed, officers barked angry orders and began to forbid this fraternization with the enemy. Soldiers who became brief friends bade adieu and returned to their own sordid trenches, the games and holidays now over, to prepare to fire upon each other once more the following day.

"No mutual kindness of this scale would happen during the Great War again," Tommy said. "By the time Christmas of 1915 rolled around, and with each successive season thereafter, the good feelings between human beings were lost. Violence begets more violence in an endless cycle. Still, though, the story of the Christmas Truce is famous for a reason. It reminds us that, though old men behind closed doors scheme for power and resources far from the frontlines, the armies they send to fight and to die are made up of living souls, fellow human beings who want to return to their homes and their families.

"Some wars have villains. The War to End All Wars had combatants, but the divides were not black or white, and all were stained with blood."

As Austin observed Tommy's consciousness, the universe around them shifted forward at a fast pace. The pair of unseen men bore witness to the entirety of the First World War in three blinks of an eye. The visual montage leaped into World War II.

Korea in the 1950s. Vietnam in the 1960s and 70s. The First and Second Gulf Wars. As noble in intent as these conflicts seemed to some and morally reprehensible to others, the core of them all was the same: aged leaders commanded the young to go forth and die for them. Sometimes for freedom. Sometimes for oil. Sometimes for a lie.

"It's a statistic that happens every time," Tommy said, sensing the direction of Austin's thoughts. "When war comes knocking, the older generations who have aged out of the draft are always in favor of fighting, often no matter how much the younger generation protests.

"Christian scripture cites wars and rumors of wars as a sign of the end of days, but it's a cryptic omen for any person of faith to interpret. There has not been a season without wars or rumors of wars, not in our recorded history, nor in the collected memories of the whole of Ascendant Beings."

"So it all comes in cycles," Austin said, closing his eyes before witnessing an act of violence in Iraq.

"Always in cycles, in a wheel that turns on and on. The cycle will continue, soon materializing itself again in a conflict between Russia and the country of Ukraine, and then spreading from there. A manifestation and distraction from the greater war of separateness that wages in the hearts of mankind."

Austin grimaced, both internally and externally, understanding suddenly that the violence he witnessed in visions of the First World War and all the rest matched that of modern wars being fought even as he attended the Institute, as he married Taylor, and enjoyed life.

"This wheel," Austin said. "Does it ever stop turning? Will it ever stop turning?"

"No," Tommy said. "It won't stop turning. It will break."

"What does that mean?"

"You've been taught by Nicholas and Vivian that the Earth is in a process of Ascension, that it moves ever onward toward its own Ascendancy. When at last it reaches that point, that is when the wheel breaks. The cycle will end. But more on that later. I have other things to show you."

Austin consciously chose not to blink, but that didn't stop everything around him from changing in an instant. The war-torn landscapes of France, Korea, Vietnam, and Ukraine were left behind, and Austin was glad to leave them. Instead, Austin now stood at the edge of a cemetery. Birds called from the many young oaks scattered through the graveyard. Morning dew had not yet left the grass. Tommy stood nearby, eyeing the proceedings of a curious funeral. The majority of the attendees wore thick masks of gauze or cheesecloth. Many wore fine clothes, suits and dresses that dated them, at Austin's guess, to sometime in the 1920s or so.

A reverend spoke from a pulpit dragged out to the graveyard. He spoke vague adages about the fragility of mortality and the tragedy of those who died young. He read generic scriptures that even Austin, who had not grown up religious, recognized from funeral scenes in movies. In the front row of the mourners, the presumed family of the deceased wept openly, their tears sinking into the gauze of their masks.

"The Spanish Flu of 1918 was a scourge on the populace of the world," Tommy said. "It infected over five hundred million people, killing well over half a million souls in the US alone."

As Austin surveyed the mourners, he spotted a familiar figure. Although he wore a mask like the rest, his features were still recognizable, as they were nearly identical to Austin's Ghost of Christmas Past.

"That's you," Austin said. "Over there. This is your hometown."

The shadow of a smile played at Tommy's mouth, but the unhappy circumstances of their visit stayed his emotions. "Yes. I attended the funeral of Billy Raymond in 1919, when the Spanish Flu still raged."

"Didn't he propose to Elsie?"

Tommy permitted a mournful smile. "He did. But his antiquated views on women held no desire for my sweet, future wife. She famously delivered him a kick that left him walking strange for days afterward."

Austin grinned, remembering the story.

"I won't deny it gave me satisfaction to see a potential revival driven away like that. But his death from the Spanish Flu was a travesty. Think about his family, Austin. He survived the Great War, returned home only to perish in his parents' house. And he wouldn't be the only one.

"A few dozen others across our humble town died of the Spanish Flu as well. The poor working conditions of the mines and the destitute circumstances of the employees did not help people's chances of survival. Many who lived suffered long-term health problems for years afterward, even the rest of their lives."

The reverend concluded his words, and the family dropped handfuls of soil into the grave of their departed son and brother.

"Your sister caught the flu, didn't she?" Austin asked.

Tommy nodded. "She did. At this very funeral, we were almost certain. The same sickness that killed Dean left my sister bedridden for days."

Austin remembered what happened next. "But you had friends in the Native Americans. They had old remedies that helped you out. And she survived."

"Yes, she did, and lived a happy life. You never knew what could happen. My own mentor, Ruby, caught the flu, but it only gave her a runny nose for a few days. Keep in mind; she was one of the oldest people in town."

"You never caught it?"

"Thankfully, no," Tommy said. "Though Elsie's father desperately hoped it would kill me."

Even as Tommy spoke, the funeral service came to an end. Some left immediately. Others mingled. An older man approached the younger Tommy and began to poke him in the chest. A young woman, clearly recognizable as Elsie, pulled at the man's arm, loudly protesting.

"There's her father now," the immortal Tommy said. "Saying it to my face, that I should have died instead of Dean. Elsie didn't speak to him for days afterward."

They young Tommy rejoined his family as they left the grave behind and returned home, parting ways with Elsie and her cruel father.

"Every generation deals with sickness," Tommy said. "Some are more devastating than others, though none have reached the heights of the Black Death in half-a-millennia. Typhus took eight million lives worldwide from 1934-1935. Your run-of-the-mill flu runs through the United States each season. It took over a hundred thousand lives in 2019. AIDS. SARS. H1N1. Zika."

Austin nodded. "And the wheel turns to the many variants of Covid-19 in the present day."

"Yes," Tommy said. "It will claim many lives by the time this year is out, with millions of recorded cases in the US alone. That sickness will pass. And after a short time, another virus will arise. It might be tamer. Or it may be worse, that is until a version of smallpox returns."

"What can I do about it?" Austin asked, visions of death and pestilence etched in his brain.

"Be prepared," was Tommy's simple reply. "Mind your physical and emotional health. Eat well. Be cautious and follow your intuition."

"But it could be unpredictable," Austin interrupted. "Like how Dean died of it, but Ruby only had minimal symptoms."

"She did," Tommy agreed. "But she was healthy for her age. But there's a chance that young Dean might not have been in that coffin over there at all if he hadn't developed a smoking habit during the war. Plagues are unpredictable, but it helps to skew the odds in your favor.

"In many ways, disease is like war. Be careful. Train yourself. Be wary of misinformation and panic. Beware of propaganda and fear mongers. If you are wise and prudent you will be fine, whatever happens."

Austin's attention returned to the now-ended funeral. Dean Masterson's family still wept and mourned at his graveside, the reverend standing stoic nearby.

"It's such a terrible cost, though," Austin whispered.

"That it certainly is," Tommy said. "Disease has claimed countlessly greater lives than any war, or all wars put together. But let's move on."

Chapter 4 -

Jazz. Drums. Lights. All of it dazzled Austin and forced him to blink. He and Tommy were in some sort of basement. Music thundered from a live band in a corner. Meanwhile, money and bottles exchanged hands between wealthy-looking people. The men all wore suits. The women kept their hair short. One even had a flapper dress on. As soon as their liquor was purchased, the patrons found a nearby table or danced to the jazz. The jovial energy of the room contained hints of anxiety and secrecy.

"It's the Roaring Twenties," Austin said.

"Yes, the time when I became a man."

"Is there something going on here? Some historically significant scene?"

"Hm?" Tommy said. "Ha. Broadly, no. I brought us here for the aesthetic while we talk about businesses in league with the government.

"See, big corporations convinced the government to outlaw alcohol—under the guise of temperance and morality—to create dependency for oil instead of the more efficient alcohol. This choice would lead to many needless oil wars over the next century.

"The federal government worked in league with big corporations to prohibit the sale, manufacture, import, or export of alcohol in 1920. Bootlegging and speakeasies flourished in every city, and well-organized criminal gangs exploded in numbers, finances, power, and influence over their respective city's politics. Corrupt politicians played into this new order, working with business owners to create a mafia style of business in the largest metropolises.

"Notably, the overall level of alcohol consumption did not go down, in part because of the wide array of speakeasies and bootlegging operations."

"I'm glad that's over, even though I don't drink much anymore," Austin said. "It seems awfully corrupt to let big corporations sway the government like that."

"It's absolutely corrupt," Tommy said. "And it's happening to this day. Government can only be so big before it becomes riddled with scandal and corruption. During this period, the Teapot Dome Scandal—in which a member of the cabinet accepted bribes from corporations—rocked the States, the most sensational scandal in America's political history up to that point."

"But there's not too much like that going on out there now," Austin said, but his confidence failed him even as he spoke. "Or is there?"

"I'm afraid there is, Austin," Tommy said. "Think of all the interactions between big businesses and governments today. Who does that serve?"

"Businesses, I guess," Austin answered.

"Exactly. And as businesses get bigger, the corruption becomes worse. These mega-corporations and their incredibly wealthy owners can take advantage of the system. Either through politically influenced legislation or indirect bribes to government officials."

"Woah," Austin said. "That's...bad."

"Very bad. It's been happening for as long as governments have existed. And it will continue to exist."

"But you were something of a billionaire in your time," Austin said. "And so is Mr. Ryan."

"I was, at least by modern standards of currency and inflation. But I recognized my purpose in this world was to serve, to teach, to bless. So has Nicholas. My wealth expanded, but it did for the purpose of aiding my fellow humans. It's not that way with all those that have great wealth, though. Not even with most of them. Absolute power has the capacity to corrupt absolutely, and greed can be a potent master over people's souls."

Chapter 5 -

"Are you familiar with unions, Austin?" Tommy asked.

Austin explained that he was familiar with the concept in a vague way, but not beyond the barest details of a high school history lesson.

"Unions," Tommy explained, "had varying degrees of influence since the Industrial Age but grew in power during the Second World War. They emerged from the conflict with temporary government bargaining, large membership, and full treasuries. Heavy industry like automobiles and steel lacked union power, but construction, printing, railroads, and other crafts had strong organization. Union membership soared during the First World War, from 2.7 million members in 1914 to five million at its peak in 1919. When unions went on strike, they had great power and influence. But corporations did fight back, and some strikes failed. This notably happened in 1919 as larger unions called for major strikes in clothing, meatpacking, steel, coal, and railroads. With this failure, union membership fell to 3.5 million members and stagnated until the passage of the Wagner Act in 1935.”

Austin found himself outside of a copper mine. Poorly-dressed workers on strike held up signs and protested poor working conditions and low wages. Police officers and federal agents surrounded the group, beating them back with truncheons. Strikers cried out in pain under the blows, but stayed firm.

“Return to work,” an officer said through a megaphone. “You are assembled unlawfully. This strike is disbanded.”

“This is awful,” Austin said.

Tommy nodded. "This strike happened in my hometown shortly after my father died in an accident in the mines. His death, among others, was one of the reasons the miner's union formed in the town and this strike took place at all."

"You weren't a part of it?'

"No. I didn't work for the mine just yet. I was doing everything I could to avoid that work. That was what my father had wanted for me, and I was doing my best to honor his wishes. As you remember, I did eventually have to work in the mine, and I hated every moment of it."

Austin watched as the feds beat at the strikers and protesters. The miners held themselves firm with resolve and determination, but their front lines wavered under the pain of the assault.

"You hated it there," Austin said. "Because working conditions were so bad."

"Abominable. This strike would eventually fail, just like many strikes before and since. Without federal intervention, I have no doubt it would have succeeded."

"But government works in league with big corporations," Austin said, understanding the direction of Tommy's thoughts.

"Indeed. The government sided with the mining company to force miners to work despite the poor conditions, which only continued to worsen with time. When I started my job in the mines, Elsie's father hoped—with decent chances—that an accident would kill me and rid him of the problems I caused."

"That's awful."

"As wages have stagnated and corporations outsource their labor to international sweatshops, unions have risen back to the forefront of headlines in your day, Austin. Unless they have become corrupted, many have, they can still be a strong advocate for their members. While you will not be directly affected by this issue, you must remember the individual. Especially in big businesses."

"Did you advocate for yourself as a miner?"

Tommy smiled sadly. "Yes…and no. The union was totally disbanded after the failed strike, so there was no formal way to do so. But I lent money judiciously to my coworkers, and that returned positive dividends as soon as I learned to do so wisely. And I got out of working in the mine as soon as I could."

"Tell me, Austin," Tommy began as the speakeasy faded into black. "Do you believe that the US is uniquely politically turbulent at this moment in time?"

"Before this duality experience, I would have said yes without thinking," Austin said. "There are huge political divides between people. But the fact that you're asking me that question means it's probably not the worst it's ever been."

Tommy laughed. "You're right. But I do want you to be right for the correct reasons, not just because you understand my teaching style.

"Take comfort in the fact that, at least for the time being, American politics are not the worst that they've ever been. The divides are sharp and bitter, but the States once divided themselves into North and South for a Civil War. The same could be said in the realm of international politics. Terrible things are happening all over the world. But there isn't a third world war just yet, and the world hasn't neared nuclear annihilation since the Cuban Missile Crisis."

"Huh," Austin said. "You're right."

"I try to be," Tommy said with a laugh. His mirth faded as his thoughts fell once again to more serious topics. "Humanity in general has the capacity to do terrible things when properly made afraid. Fear fosters atrocities. A populace manipulated into terror by its leaders is potentially moldable to the will of authority.

"That is why the majority of political maneuvering revolves around deception and fear mongering. Politicians and the elite will bring up concerns and often exaggerate them to manipulate their constituents into supporting their agendas. Whole movements can be created in response to these manufactured fears."

"But they can't all be fake," Austin said. "No one would vote for you if you tried to make people scared of fake things."

"Yes…and no," Tommy said.

History passed before Austin in the twinkle of an eye. The Red Scares flashed before him. Isolated pockets of communism sparked nationwide terror of secret Stalinists hiding among the Americans. Bombings in Wall Street and the May Day Riots served to heighten these fears. Before long, any voice critical of the government, or anyone with leftist sympathies became suspect. The House Un-American Activities Committee, or HUAC, was formed to investigate alleged disloyalty among American citizenry and companies. Joseph McCarthy rose to power amid the witch hunts for suspected communists. Art began to reflect these concerns in turn; horror and science fiction media revolved around spies, communists, and frightening aliens who could be anyone—your next door neighbor, your friend, even your spouse. Hollywood had a blacklist that forbade employment for suspected communist sympathizers.

"Some fears weaponized by politicians are so inane as to be, essentially, fiction. Other times, the global elite take something small and magnify it, exaggerate it into a national threat that needs to be dealt with. And sometimes the fear is something very real and worth addressing, though in my experience those instances are rare."

In the South, Austin witnessed fear and racial separation following the Civil War. The Ku Klux Klan formed to frighten and create more of a sense of racism and separateness. Politicians weaponized the Temperance Movement to pass Prohibition.

"You will see that religion and race have had a profound effect on politics," Tommy said, voice mournful. "Religion can be good, but it ceases to serve humanity when the structure becomes a god to be worshiped."

Austin nodded. Given recent history, that was not a difficult idea for the two men to agree on.

Chapter 6 -

"You have homosexual friends, Austin, correct?"

"Yeah, I do," Austin said, used to the quick pace and shifting of topics in his conversations with Mr. Ryan. He thought about Talia. The former Israeli military pilot had come out to her friends at the Institute as lesbian a long while ago. She sometimes struggled to reconcile her sexuality with her family's expectations. And while Marti, the chef's assistant at the Institute, had never said anything, Austin suspected he might be gay.

Tommy sensed the direction of his thoughts and nodded. "It's not an easy road them, and it's not often one that they chose."

"Did you know any people in your time that were attracted to the same gender?" Austin asked.

Tommy nodded. "Miles Bertrum grew up with me. We didn't have the terminology to call him gay, not back then. We didn't notice anything different about him for a long time. He tried his best to play baseball and be one of the guys, but he was far more inclined to book reading. He was a poet. He wasn't interested in the girls like the rest of us, never went on a date his parents didn't force on him. While he wasn't good at baseball, Elsie and I still liked him; he was too kind to dislike. But as we grew older, the other boys—and his father—sensed differences about him. They bullied him mercilessly. Called him a fairy. His father was desperate to make him heterosexual."

Austin hadn't forgotten the context in which Miles's name had come up. "But then he went to the war."

"Then he went to the war," Tommy repeated. "Had Miles survived, he would have made a remarkable poet, a powerful member of the Lost

Generation of writers. But mustard gas took him a month after he arrived on the front.

"You've been told time and again that the reality of the world is an illusion. It creates a façade of separation between groups. Us and them. Organized religion in America has largely fallen for the lie of separation, even though we are all one and the same. It's more of the illusion of separation. And it's a continuation of the cycle. There's always a marginalized group, and the same rhetoric is used against these groups every time. Think of the holocaust of World War II.

"But that brings me to my next point. The Earth is in the process of ascending. The wheel turns, but as Ascension nears, a lot of things improve. The standard of living has increased exponentially. So has technological expansion. Life expectancy rises as infant mortality rates lower. With greater Ascension comes the uniting of people of all differences. Race, gender, etc. The rejection of all isms."

"Wait a minute, though," Austin said. "Issues of genderism and racism are still a big thing today."

"True," Tommy conceded. "But those issues are increasingly rejected by mainstream culture. It will continue that way until the cycle stops and the wheel breaks."

Austin longed to ask about this breaking of the wheel, but he sensed Tommy's thoughts and teachings going in a different direction for the time being.

The scene faded to dark. Austin felt some discomfort in the void of blackness. While he'd had duality experiences with Nicholas before, he didn't enjoy the sensation of seeing nothing even with his eyes open.

Tommy ended his discomfort by constructing a vision before them. A giant, marble statue of a human woman towered over them, her back to the pair of men.

"This statue of a human woman," Tommy said. "What race do you suppose she is a member of?"

Austin squinted. "I can't tell. Does it matter?"

The statue rotated to reveal a woman with Asian features.

"No," Tommy said. "It absolutely does not matter."

Austin couldn't hold back just a hint of frustration. "Then why did you ask me about it at all?"

"Because, almost exclusively for the worse, humanity has had too great a fixation on race," Tommy said. As he spoke, the statue before them changed repeatedly in height, weight, race, body shape, and gender. Polynesian man. White woman. Southeast Asian woman. Inuit man. "This viewpoint has justified endless crimes—the peculiar institution of slavery across thousands of years. Dehumanization of entire cultures and civilizations. Genocide. Even today, the belief that race determines meaningful things about you as a person permeates societies."

"But race does determine some things about you," Austin said. "My friend Grace is African American. And that simple fact has influenced her home and family culture, her upbringing, her religion. And that's true for me, too, as a white man. The same goes for Talia. She's Jewish. Or Meeki. She's Korean."

"That's true," Tommy conceded. "Race has historically affected us as human beings. And it's imperative that we know and understand that history, the good and the bad. But when it comes down to it, race and ethnicity do not matter."

"Not at all?" Austin asked.

"Not at all. Fixation on race is a distraction. It was first crafted by a small group with nefarious intentions long ago to divide groups and individuals from one another. The world would be a better place if that had never happened. We could have simply acknowledged and perhaps even treasured our differences in ideas, thought, and culture, instead of using the quantity of skin pigmentation to determine who oppresses whom."

"That's really sad," Austin said.

"It really is," Tommy agreed. "Especially because race is literally skin-deep. Race does not cause any meaningful biological difference. It's a matter of pigmentation and nothing more. And yet society has a hard time letting it go."

"I wish we could," Austin said.

"It's complicated," Tommy added. "While we need to let go of the divisive nature of race, we have to come to terms with ancestry and history, too. Healing from generational trauma can't happen until we do."

Austin remembered his friend, Joseph. His ancestors had been involved in an atrocity known as the Mountain Meadows Massacre in the western United States in 1857. That history had nothing to do with race. But Tommy's principle rang true to Austin's heart; because Joseph's family had never fully confronted this part of their history, the generational trauma persisted, manifesting in Joseph's dreams and nightmares.

Tommy waited as Austin related the ideas to his and his friends' experiences, then spoke. "And the greatest tragedy is that racist atrocities are often crimes against ourselves. Not just in the sense that we all live in an illusion of separation, but also in that we can live in different lifetimes and different bodies."

"What do you mean?" Austin asked.

"The singular spirit body can dwell in different physical bodies throughout time. Your own prime spirit has endured multiple lifetimes and thousands of partial lifetimes. Some bodies even host multiple composite spirits at the same moment in linear time."

Austin knew his question was bold, but he decided the worst that Tommy could do is refuse him. "Could you tell me a little about my past lifetimes?"

Tommy thought for a moment. "Yes. You once lived in India a very long time ago. And as a Native

83

American in the early nineteenth century. You've even lived on different planets, where you were a member of a blue-skinned race, a phenotype that the Hindus would recall from Shiva."

"Wait," Austin said. "What about my experience as a Native American? Can you tell me more about that one?" His curiosity was piqued at the idea of being a blue alien, but he sensed something important about his Native American lifetime.

"Your most recent previous life," Tommy said, reaching to it with his consciousness. "It's not a happy experience. It was the mid-1800s. You lived just over twenty-five years, before European settlers killed you as you defended your home, your people, and important ancient records. You weren't of the right race. You weren't of the right nationality. So you were a victim of a terrible genocide. If you try, you can reach out and sense that lifetime within you."

Austin wasn't certain that he wanted to try, knowing that the end of that previous life would be only pain and suffering, but he did as Tommy instructed. First, he processed the information his mentor had given him. Then he reached out with his mind.

A torrent of memories returned to him in scattered fragments and tears, flashes like déjà vu. He remembered his mother. His grandfather. His tribe and people. Alliances. Treaties. Betrayals. War.

Austin had believed Tommy's words before. But this idea of remortalization had been just that: an idea. An entertaining and fascinating one, even. But as the broken pieces of another life invaded Austin's mind, he knew it was all true.

One fragment fascinated him in particular as he sorted through a million thoughts, ideas, and emotions long forgotten.

"Taylor…" Austin whispered, more a statement than a question.

"You see her," Tommy said.

"Yes. She was there, too."

"At your side to the end. She did not live much longer than you."

Austin nodded, tears stinging his eyes as he vicariously experienced the bitter despair of his past life and his past people.

"You two are quite something," Tommy continued. "You've known each other more than just the past few years in this lifetime. Your relationship with her goes back tens of thousands of years."

Austin recognized the truth as images and memories soaked with emotion streamed through his awareness. As much as he wanted to stop and isolate them, though, he knew this was a brief tangent in his duality experience.

"Direct racism did not play a notable role in my most recent lifetime," Tommy continued. "Our little town had no notion of modern ideas of diversity, racial or otherwise. It was, to my memory, almost exclusively white. But we read things in the newspapers, and later heard things on the radio.

"The culture war between different groups raged elsewhere. Cities were relatively peaceful, with a few large-scale race riots. But widespread confrontations did take place. 1943 saw a race riot in Detroit, and Los Angeles bore witness to the anti-Mexican Zoot Suit Riots. The Second World War would also see Japanese Americans interned in concentration camps. Their ancestry made them suspected enemies and traitors.

"The Klan had diminished over time, its reputation eroded by overt racism. It's now been replaced with more the thought of anti-racism. Though that idea in and of itself is also racist by its very existence, still buying into the lie that we are all separate."

"But won't that change as the planet ascends?" Austin asked.

"Absolutely." Tommy's cheerful countenance returned. "Yes. Racism isn't gone yet. But when at last the wheel breaks, that will mark the end of racism, too. Humanity will live in harmony because they will see through the illusions of separation."

It was a comforting thought for Austin.

Chapter 7 -

"Is Taylor a person, Austin? Is she a human being?"

"Yes, of course," Austin answered. The question and its answer were simple, but Austin played along, knowing that the lesson was entering a new direction.

"Does Taylor as a woman merit the same rights and liberties that you possess as a man?"

"Yes," Austin said. "Though I know that hasn't always been the case.

"No," Tommy said. "And you've picked up on the direction of our discussion. Sexism has been a part of many humans' mindsets and limiting beliefs since time immemorial. Even though Plato and Socrates lived as the greatest minds of their people and day, even they fell victim to baggage and limiting beliefs; they fully and wholeheartedly believed that women were subhuman, animalistic in nature compared to the nobler minds of men."

"I didn't know that," Austin said, eyes wide. "That's horrible."

"It really, really is," Tommy agreed. "But the wheel—"

"Has turned, and the cycle has continued," Austin interrupted. "Things have improved for women with time as the Earth Ascends."

"Correct."

Colors blurred and shapes changed. Austin and Tommy watched a baseball game among children. It didn't take much thought for Austin to guess where they were.

"This is your childhood," he said. "This is one of your baseball games."

"It certainly is," Tommy said, a nostalgic bend to his smile. "I couldn't count how many games we played. So many victories. So many losses. High emotions and high stakes for a game played in the dirt."

The pair of men watched as one of the young boys, doubtless Miles Bertram, earned three strikes. He trudged away from home base, head downward.

Nearby, a little girl approached the game on light feet. But the nearest boys waved their arms at her, stopping her. Austin couldn't hear what they said, but he knew they were forbidding a young Elsie from participating in their game.

"This wouldn't be the first time that Elsie understood that being a girl put her in a different place in society," Tommy said. "Baseball was a game just for boys, so they forbade her from joining."

The young boy Tommy departed briefly from the game to console his friend. She held back her tears, but Elsie's disappointment at another rejection was evident in the slump of her shoulders and the limpness of her arms at her sides.

That was when a bat struck the ball. It sailed high and away, landing in a distant, well-manicured garden. Even from their distance, Austin heard the children groan in fear and dismay. He recalled from the story that the faraway yard belonged to Ruby McLellan, the old widow with sour feelings toward children. It was fascinating to watch events he knew so well play out in living color.

As the children quivered at the idea of fetching their ball from the yard of the local terror, Elsie and Tommy hatched their scheme. Elsie would go and fetch the ball. This would provide the street cred Elsie needed to earn a spot she so desired playing baseball. The act of immense bravery and valor worked, though the young girl used a tactic that had never occurred to the boys. Rather than darting in and out of the frightening woman's yard for the ball, she instead approached casually. When Ruby emerged from the house to tell the child to get off her property, Elsie greeted her and offered to do a few chores around the yard over the weekend, including pulling weeds from among the roses that Ruby loved. Ruby agreed, and it marked the beginning of a friendship that would define the rest of their lives and Tommy's as well.

"That was a clever plan," Austin said. "She never would have been able to play if this hadn't happened."

"Ruby and Elsie both were powerful women," Tommy said. "While they both grew up in a world shaped and run by men, they both managed to game the system in their own ways, allowing them rights and privileges they otherwise would not have possessed. Elsie displayed bravery greater than that of the boys around her. While Ruby was a widow, she maintained influence over her late husband's business holdings throughout her life. She would allow Elsie and I into her life, first to do chores, then to read with her in her library, a then unprecedented luxury in the town. When we came of age, Elsie and I became involved in Ruby's business dealings, where she prepared us for a world of money and politics, and all the while she helped shape Elsie into someone who could play the system of men into her favor beyond children's baseball diamonds.

"But Elsie met with much opposition from home. Marshall, her father, was a man mired in tradition. He put up with Elsie's reading, even though he distrusted the written word, because of the connection it provided to Ruby McLellan and, quite possibly, her wealth. He hoped to be written into Ruby's will because of her friendship with Elsie.

"It was a two-edged sword for old Marshall, though. Because while he approved of time spent with Ruby, he didn't like the influence he felt I had on Elsie."

"What did you do that Marshall disliked so much?" Austin asked.

"Nothing I regret, that's for certain. I encouraged Elsie's reading habits, and discussed the idea of education with her. And Elsie had her own good head on her shoulders, so she balked at a lot of her father's views. Because of his limited views on women, he actually gave me more credit for his daughter's rebellious nature than I deserved.

"In the end, Marshall Miller died a sad and lonely old man, with a funeral attended by few and mourned by even fewer. I was the only speaker for the service. While the cause of his death was a stroke, it came about because of his buried emotions. Marshall maintained a lifetime's worth of negative emotions locked deep in his body, where it stayed until his physical being simply couldn't handle it anymore."

"Just like I said to Nicholas," Austin said. "He died of being a jerk."

Tommy laughed. "In some ways I suppose he did. He was a victim of a deeply traditional family that passed that mindset down to him. And while that doesn't absolve Marshall of his wrongs, it does provide insight into how and why he functioned. Women belonged exclusively in the domestic sphere. By force of tradition, not by free will. Many women live as housewives. They raise children, work in the house, labor in kitchens and gardens. And that's wonderful, something to be celebrated…when they do it because that's what they want."

"Absolutely," Austin said. He couldn't imagine being the "boss" of Taylor, ordering her around. She was very much his equal in their matrimony. In terms of growth and personal development, she'd excelled beyond him with the bite of a single fruit.

Austin had difficulty imagining the frustration of being a woman in Elsie and Ruby's time. The two women lived in a country in which they had no representation in their own government, where husbands and fathers controlled most every aspect of their lives, from their finances to their weddings to their clothing. Remarkable women held sway and sometimes even changed the world, and their actions were not to be demeaned or forgotten, but Elsie and Ruby both, despite living through mostly different periods of history, ultimately spent much of their lives as second-class citizens.

It wasn't until 1920 that women obtained the right to vote in all state and federal elections through the passage of the Nineteenth Amendment. With this new right, women's issues actually mattered and influenced elections. Politicians responded to the abrupt arrival of a massive new electorate–approximately half of the population suddenly gaining suffrage–by emphasizing issues of special interest to women.

Women would also go on to join the workforce in unprecedented numbers to replace the men who had gone off to fight in the Second World War, their symbol the long iconic Rosie the Riveter. This led to massive changes in the roles of women in society. The war ended, but not all women abandoned the workforce.

But there was a world out there that, in some areas and in some regards, still viewed Taylor as a lesser human than Austin by mere virtue of their sex. There were still nations and regions where women had no say in their lives or their governments.

"Geez," Austin said. "I don't know how they handle it."

"Sometimes I don't either," Tommy said. "Elsie dealt with a great deal of sexism in our time. We all too often had visits from business associates and journalists who spoke only to me, all but ignoring her outside of polite introductions. Elsie almost always had to assert herself into interviews and business meetings or risk being cut out of negotiations altogether."

"Didn't you help her?"

"I did what I could, and I did what Elsie asked of me. She rarely needed my help, though. She enjoyed asserting herself as a sort of power play to surprise people, and it just about always worked. I wish she hadn't needed to do that, though. It lasted our entire mortal lifetime. But, the wheel turns and the cycle happens as it happens. Your Taylor has found a

better world for women than the one Ruby and later
Elsie were born into. And things will continue to
change and improve."

Chapter 8 -

Austin blinked, and he and his mentor were suddenly floating in a sea of ever changing numbers and codes. He reached out to touch a floating number two, but his hand passed through it.

"This is awesome," Austin said. "Like we're in the Matrix."

"I'm afraid our next topic isn't quite as entertaining as that," Tommy said. "We're here to discuss debt."

"Oh," Austin said. He had a history of debt from his weaker days, a pileup of bills and loans from online gambling, going out to eat too much, and unnecessary gaming purchases. It had gotten bad enough that his parents cut him off financially. It had been one of the hardest periods of his life, one he only made it through with wisdom and skills gained from

Nicholas Ryan and the Institute. Even now, though, Austin still had some student loans to pay off. He was more aware than most of the pitfalls of borrowing money.

Tommy chuckled at the sheepish emotion emanating from Austin. "It's quite all right to be a little embarrassed at past mistakes, as long as you come to terms with them and eventually let them go.

"Debt is a dangerous thing, something to be treated very carefully. One should avoid debt for frivolous things such as fancy cars or some unneeded, newfangled technology. If used unwisely, it can create slavery, and ruin lives and relationships."

Austin nodded. Even though he'd never been in too much financial danger, even when his parents cut him off, he understood how the stress of money woes could take a toll on a person's mental and physical health. Odds were, he figured, that Tommy understood that feeling even more than he did.

"Did you ever have any debt?" Austin asked.

"Stop me if this sounds familiar, but…"

"Yes and no," Austin said, smiling and rolling his eyes good-naturedly.

"Yes and no," Tommy agreed. "I never incurred any unnecessary debts myself, but my family did. I worked in the copper mines in part to pay those old dues off for good. So while those debts may not have officially been my own, they were functionally mine.

"I hated every moment I worked in the misery of those mines, and I didn't even have it the worst of anyone there. The conditions and pay were so poor that many of my coworkers were in debt to the mining company itself. To help my comrades out, I started lending money here and there, charging a much lower interest than they'd find anywhere else. The first time I did it was a disaster. The man took my money and ran. But I lent more judiciously after that, and helped others get out of potentially lifelong debts while making myself a small profit.

"The Great Depression was a time of debt. For farmers, it was even before then. Many families mortgaged their farms in the 1920s to provide money to…get through until better times. Little did they know of the harder times to come. Most of these farms were foreclosed when the families couldn't make the payments.

"On a national scale, debt can be dangerous. Germany's defeat at the end of the Great War left the country mired in debts and reparation payments to its former enemies. The harshness of these reparations, all part of the Treaty of Versailles that marked the end of the war, led in part to the rise of Hitler and his nationalism. Debt hasn't been any kinder to the US. It's been an issue since the nation's founding. Debt soared under President Hoover in my time, and it only increased during the Second World War."

"And that's the cycle," Austin said. "Debt is back to the forefront of discourse."

"Exactly. Whichever political party isn't in power criticizes the other for its spending habits, despite having similar ambitions for their own agendas. For politicians, debt is a tool to be used against opponents, not a real issue they have to personally worry about. But the US has a big spending problem, a deficit, spending more money than it makes.

"For individuals debt has become a form of subconscious slavery. It's designed to keep you in its grasp for life, a terrible cycle encouraged by cultural norms and shaped by powerful entities."

Austin nodded, understanding the seriousness of the information.

"But let's turn to happier times," said Tommy. "I was privileged to live as a young man in the 1920s."

"But that's right before the Depression," Austin said. "It didn't stay happy."

"It certainly did not. But that's how the cycle goes, particularly for the economy. Good times are followed by bad times, then good times return, and so forth. That was especially true for me in the 1920s. Some of the best and worst days of my life happened in that window. While Elsie left for college–in part because she wanted an education, and in part because her father wanted her away from me–I became Ruby's travel assistant, going with her to visit her late husband's business holdings and meet with his partners. I learned the finer workings of business and met lifelong friends and connections during those travels." Tommy's smile faded. "But the wheel turned. My father died in a mining accident, and before long I was slaving away in the very same caverns where he perished."

"But you got to marry Elsie eventually," Austin said. "The wheel turned in your favor after a while."

"It did. I have not forgotten. And she has been the joy of my existence, both before and after Ascendancy."

Austin blinked, and when his eyes opened, he stared at an old New York City skyline, doubtless the cityscape of the 1920s. There were fewer towers and skyscrapers, which made those present all the more imposing and breathtaking. This was a period of American prosperity in almost all sectors of life, though agriculture and coal mining suffered. But construction flourished as factories, office buildings, paved roads, and new housing came to be. Automobile production soared. Suburban housing expanded. Electricity came into the city and people's homes.

"Yes," Tommy said. "It was quite something to travel with Ruby across the country and see this nation in such a state, especially given my own humble origins. It was a period of new industries and new technology. President Coolidge famously declared that 'the business of America is business.'"

"Nobody saw the crash coming?" Austin asked. "It seems so obvious."

"Well, you know what they say about hindsight being 20/20," Tommy said. "And it's awfully easy to be a Monday night quarterback. Some suspected that there was something coming. Others prepared for the worst, not out of a sense of fear, but out of a need to be ready."

"People like you and Elsie?"

"Yes. I won't lie, though, it was easy for a lot of people to get caught up in the magic of all that prosperity. Elsie even had to snap me out of it and get us back on track. But the signs were there. Credit was extended to a dangerous degree, including in the stock market, which rose to the highest levels of the time. Inflation was high and interest rates were low. People spent freely with cheap cash flowing and illegal booze pouring. Stocks and bonds were up at the same time. It was all dangerously inflated."

Tommy went on to explain the workings of the time. "Energy," he said, "speared the economy forward, electricity and oil in particular. New advances in technology led to new and growing demands. People's homes and workplaces had electricity, so soon they had light bulbs, refrigerators, toasters, and other increasingly modern appliances. Meanwhile, the US dominated petroleum production the world over, with oil booms in California, Oklahoma, and Texas. This development aided the economy even more, as the age of automobiles and trucks had arrived.

"This prosperity won Hoover the presidency, but the resulting economic downturn betrayed him, and he lost in a landslide to Franklin Roosevelt."

Chapter 9 -

Tommy next lifted them away to somewhere somewhat familiar to Austin. It was a humble little town, Tommy's own place of birth, where he spent his boyhood. Although Austin had been there once with Nicholas and Taylor, that was in the present. Elsie's library did not yet dominate the town. No doubt it was still a tiny bookshop in the back of the general store.

"What year is it?" Austin asked.

"It's 1930," Tommy said. "In the time of the Great Depression."

Austin recalled history lessons, both from school and the Institute, that touched on the Depression. Stocks and bonds were both going up in 1929, now a recognized warning sign of a corrective event. After the stock market crashed, American jobs and employment took a historic tumble. The US dollar deflated terribly. Unemployment skyrocketed from 3% to 25%. Manufacturing output collapsed by a third. Unable to support their families, many men deserted their families to live in so-called "Hoovervilles"—shantytowns built by the destitute—so that the meager supplies that they left behind for their families could be stretched further. People lost their life savings as banks collapsed one after the other. The federal government intervened with a bank holiday by way of the Emergency Banking Act.

Recovery from the Depression was torturously slow, despite government efforts to restart the economy. But with no major new industries in the 30s big enough to drive growth the way that autos, electricity, and construction previously had, there was no driving force to help heal the economy. The droughts and heat waves caused by the Dust Bowl only heightened American misery. A renewed recession would hit in 1937. Roosevelt instituted numerous social programs. Among the more successful initiatives to relieve citizens included the Civilian Conservation Corps, the Civil Works Administration, and the Federal Emergency Relief Administration. It would take the beginning of the Second World War to jumpstart everything again, and the US GDP surpassed levels from 1929 in 1940.

But as Austin observed the town, he didn't see any hallmarks of the Depression. No bread lines, no long lines for potential jobs. The people who walked by seemed in decent, even high spirits.

"I don't understand," Austin said.

"What's unclear?" Tommy asked.

"This town…it doesn't look like the Great Depression."

"Oh? How so?" Tommy asked even though he knew the direction of Austin's thoughts.

"Where are the soup kitchens? The long lines? The closed banks?"

"Ah." Tommy nodded. "My humble little hometown stayed safe during the Depression."

"That's right." Austin remembered. "You were prepared."

"Elsie and I were prepared," Tommy said, a subtle correction. "While we didn't predict the future, we kept in good communication with our Higher Power and sought it out for answers. That provided us with good guidance. We also had savings; Elsie and I had invested diversely and wisely. When we had the funds and influence, I took over the local bank as well as three local farms. I created a co-op to help farmers get better prices. Employment was dangerously high. People were desperate for whatever work they could find. We had the resources to keep our people paid and taken care of even as we made a profit. We were extremely fortunate. And extremely prepared.

"Economies are not always predictable, but their big picture movements are. It moves like a wave. Take on behaviors similar to ours here, and you can weather the economic difficulties of your own future."

Austin agreed. "Save yourself. Then save others."

"Exactly."

"Will it ever be as bad as the Great Depression again?" Austin asked.

"Probably. Economies shift but the patterns remain the same. But even when it's as bad as the Great Depression or worse, you can still use these tools and this knowledge. First for yourself and then to help others in your sphere of influence."

"Another thing about my time," continued Tommy. "Big government passed dubious or outright unconstitutional laws. If it couldn't be passed as law through Congress, the president made it an executive order. Propaganda manipulated and obligated people into compliance without them realizing what was going on."

Austin remembered a similar conversation with Nicholas in his early days at the Institute. He'd believed that propaganda was a thing of the past, a wartime relic. In his head, it was little more than Disney cartoon characters and comic book heroes fighting Nazis and Uncle Sam wanting YOU to join the US army. Nicholas had all but scoffed at Austin's ignorance, explaining that propaganda still existed, even flourished, in the modern day. People missed it because it was far more insidious and subtle than the jingoistic posters and war footage of yesteryear. In the digital age, propaganda crept its way into your social media feed whether you knew it or not. Algorithms picked up on your preferences and interests, from little things like your fashion sense and favorite food to potentially more private things, like your political leanings, sexual orientation, and purchase history. Social media collected this information and sold it to companies to better target you with their advertising. This guileful method yielded such harmless results as an ad for a cheeseburger the algorithm knew you liked. But it also created dangerous political echo chambers, confirming and feeding your own biases back to you.

Tommy mournfully closed his eyes along with Austin as they considered that danger. "Propaganda only increases in dangerous times. This is true for big government, as well. In times of crisis, emergency powers are granted to the authority. It is rare that those powers are ever relinquished once given."

"Just like in the *Star Wars* movies!" Austin said. "When Jar Jar Binks gets the Galactic Senate to grant emergency powers to the Supreme Chancellor. He became the emperor because of that."

"I…suppose that's an example," Tommy said, somewhat bemused. "It's a truth that goes back to Ancient Rome. Powerful men became temporary dictators to save the empire from crisis. Only rarely did they step down once the disaster was averted. It applies to American history as well. Abraham Lincoln saved the Union, but in so doing, he expanded the powers of the executive branch past the intention of the Founding Fathers, for good and for ill. Roosevelt did the same during the Depression and the Second World War. Among other things, he seized private business–similar to mine–to be controlled by the government. He also tried to pack the Supreme Court to push through his agendas."

"That's definitely happening today," Austin said. "Both sides of the aisle are desperate to skew the courts to their side."

"Precisely, and both are guilty of utilizing underhanded, diabolical, and hypocritical tactics to make it happen." Tommy sighed. "It wasn't good. In the meantime, taxes and whether or not to increase them became contentious."

"That's happening today, too," Austin groaned. "Some people want to cut taxes on the rich. Others want to tax them more."

"The wheel turns–"

"And history moves in cycles," Austin finished for Tommy. "It feels like we just keep making the same old mistakes."

Tommy laughed, but there wasn't much humor in it. "That's because we do, Austin. Technology

changes and develops. Empires rise and fall. But
human nature stays much the same, and our collective
memory is remarkably short."

Chapter 10 -

The two men stood high above the ocean. The Pacific glittered beneath them, its wavy surface marred by the smoke of war. WWII-era battleships engaged in perilously close quarters, destroyers firing on one another. Planes launched into the firmament from aircraft carriers, flying complex maneuvers as they sought and destroyed enemy fighters. One side waved American banners, the other the rising sun of Japan. Austin could only hear the faintest booms of the guns and cannons from this distance. He was grateful for that separation; after bearing witness to the rages of several wars, he had no desire to see further violence so close.

"This," Tommy said, "is the Battle of Midway. My son was drafted into the navy. He would have fought here, but he contracted a bad case of cholera and never saw combat."

"Oh, I've seen some movies about this," Austin said. "This is when the US started to win the war with Japan. It's considered one of the most decisive naval battles in military history."

Tommy nodded. "World War Two began in Europe in 1938. Note that that's a Shmita year, ending after a cycle of seven years."

"But the US didn't join the war until later," Austin said. "Not until after the attack on Pearl Harbor in December of 1941. And the Battle of Midway happened something like six months later."

"Ah, a World War II scholar," Tommy said.

Austin grinned. "I….I don't know. I had a phase in high school."

"Then you may not be as familiar with the home front affairs," Tommy said. "The US did not engage directly in the war for some time, like you said. The States preferred to serve in a supportive, indirect role that left them neutral in theory, if not in practice. Still, the US limited itself to providing supplies and weapons to Britain, China, and the Soviet Union by way of the Lend-Lease program. Of course, this action did not sit well with the Axis Powers. Japan would later feel provoked into attacking Pearl Harbor, leading to the United States' formal entry into the war.

"Italy surrendered in 1943, followed by Germany and Japan in 1945. The war took a Great Depression-era economy and created a massive industrial mobilization, affecting American society more than any other armed conflict, except maybe the Civil War."

"You were part of that," Austin said. "That economic boom."

"Indeed I was. Like we've talked, the government eventually began to buy my materials at a much higher rate than expected. I was wealthy by then, but that deal made me into a millionaire. I saw an opportunity, one that could help me and help others, and took it."

"How did you know that would work?"

"I didn't, not completely. But Elsie and I appealed to our Higher Power and sought guidance. We made reasonably intelligent and informed guesses based on the information we had. And it worked. Of course, the wartime economy helped us out a lot, with or without government contracts. While many goods like meat and metal were tightly rationed for the war, America experienced tightly controlled prices and wages. American citizens saved up more money than they did before. This led to renewed growth after the war instead of a return to the Depression."

The battle of Midway raged on beneath them. Austin was sure it was his imagination, but he thought he could hear the screams of dying men below. He shuddered.

"Will something like this happen again?" he asked.

"Perhaps one day," Tommy said. "The nuclear arms race that followed the bombings of Hiroshima and Nagasaki have kept the wars of super-powered nations to smaller scales and foreign theaters, but it may not always be able to stay that way. Still, we have reason to hope that as the world's Ascension continues, that war itself will one day come to an end."

"1945 marked the end of an era," Tommy continued. "The former world powers diminished, and the US became the new superpower, equipped with advanced technology and a thriving economy. The US has made itself a powerful and far-reaching empire with a self-proclaimed right to police the world. Its membership in the United Nations, a marked difference from its absence in the League of Nations, granted this boldness some degree of legitimacy. The end of the Second World War had birthed an entirely new world reshaped from the old, never to be the same again.”

“It's been a long time, though,” Austin said. “The US is starting to lose its status as the world power.”

Tommy smiled. “It really hasn't been so long. But I can understand that it seems that way from your perspective. You are correct, though, that the United States as a superpower has begun to wane. And that's–”

“Part of the cycle.”

"Yes. You've got it. It has been seventy-seven years, or eleven sets of seven, since 1945. It is time for the wheel to turn as it always does. Another nation could take its place as leader of the world, for good or for ill."

"What will we do if that does happen?" Austin said. It occurred to him that he hadn't ever lived outside a global superpower before.

"You just keep living," Tommy said simply. "Most of the world doesn't live in the United States, and they've somehow managed it for a lifetime. It may be messy, but many will make it through."

Chapter 11 -

"Tommy," Austin said. "How many Ascendant Beings are there?"

"Many. Exceedingly many, though I suppose our numbers are pitifully few in proportion to the rest of the planet. There are Ascendant Beings walking this world as we speak who have lived seven prime lifetimes and longer."

Frustration curled somewhere in Austin's gut. "You've shown me so many things, Mr. Campbell."

"Call me Tommy, please."

Austin smiled despite the churning of his thoughts and emotions. "Tommy. I feel like I've seen and experienced so many of the worst things that history has to offer. You've shown me war, disease, corruption, greed, all kinds of evil perpetrated by humankind. Ascendant Beings like you are so powerful and so good. So pure. Why aren't they doing more?"

"You don't think we do enough?" Tommy asked.

Austin thought before answering. "To quote you a few times during these lessons: yes…and no. You and Elsie achieved so much. The two of you created jobs, ran charities, promoted literacy. But I feel like so many people up high like you spend their time doing chores or pondering the secrets of the universe. Why not be leaders?"

"Ah." Tommy said. "I understand. Ascendancy…comes with its own difficulties. When you see so much truth, it's easy to elevate yourself above other people, whether out of pride or out of a simple inability to relate to regular humans. We withdraw, because in too many ways, we're not precisely human ourselves anymore."

"But the purpose of Ascendant Beings is to bless, teach, and serve," Austin said. "Like what you did."

"It is," Tommy acknowledged. "But we souls exist to have joy also. Ascendant Beings are allowed to enjoy themselves."

"That's not the problem," Austin said. "I just feel like so many of the Ascendant Beings I've met spend their time on remote mountain tops and at mystery schools."

"And that's bad?"

"No," Austin replied. "But also…yes. Pondering the secrets of the universe and teaching them to the people who seek you out is noble and all that, but…you just showed me the worst of humanity, Tommy. Ascendant Beings have the power to do something about all those bad things, and they don't."

"I see." Tommy stared at the modern Earth and its too-brown surface. "Why don't we intervene more in the affairs of humanity?"

"Yeah, exactly."

Tommy sighed. "I wish I had a better answer, Austin. People Ascend. They seek more knowledge. They seek a purpose. When they find one, they pursue it. But the lone and dreary world is vast and teeming with endless billions of people. Even we could feel overwhelmed at the prospect of changing it all. Sometimes it is easier to spend one's immortality going to mystery schools, mastering nature, and teaching your skills to willing students.

"I will leave you with this comfort, Austin. You are right. It's not quite enough. Earlier in this lesson, you asked me when the wheel would stop turning, when the historical cycles would end. That time is nearing. I can't—and won't—tell you exactly when it will happen. But the wheel will break soon, and it will be in your lifetime."

Austin's eyes widened. "Will it, uh…break in a good way?"

"It certainly won't be easy." Tommy closed his eyes, as if to protect himself from unwanted visions. "When it happens, it will be preceded by exceedingly difficult times. But yes, in the end, the wheel will break 'in a good way.' The cycle will finally come to an end. The Earth will be allowed to Ascend to a paradisiacal state."

"What will it take to do that?" Austin asked.

"You actually came close to guessing it yourself. It does not have to be this way, but the hard times or intentional choices shape mighty people into heroic figures and leaders. A few people will Ascend, greater than all the Ascendant Beings that came before them. And they will be greater because they will do what the others have not–by intervening directly into world affairs, while still honoring individual agency. They will use their power to end separations and sufferings and help usher in the Ascendancy of the Earth."

"Oh," Austin said, unable to find words to describe what he was hearing.

"It's sure to be an interesting time," Tommy said. "But, alas, our time together is coming to a close." Even though Austin knew Tommy wasn't tired, the Ascendant man wiped at his brow to mimic the emotion he knew Austin was experiencing. "How are you feeling?"

Austin didn't answer immediately. Emotions—not all of them his own, or from his lifetime—boiled in his brain. It was almost overwhelming, both how much history he had witnessed, and the knowledge that those basic patterns would repeat for him.

"There's so much." Austin couldn't keep the awe out of his voice. "What should I do?"

"You don't need to remember every facet of history," Tommy said. "Just remember the main ideas behind what you've seen today. These are patterns. They have repeated for nations and empires, going back thousands of years. That means that even though you'll never know all the details of the future, you can look at the writing on the wall and predict these patterns. Pay attention to the cycles. Three-and-a-half years. Seven years. Seventy years. Three hundred and forty-three years.

"I won't tell you everything I know, but know that if this pattern follows true, there will be a major economic downturn for the country, followed by the rest of the world, some two years from now."

Austin rubbed his temples with his hands.

"Don't panic, Austin. It's not necessarily a bad thing. Economies flow. It's a matter of perspective. And besides, you have the tools and knowledge to make it. Do what Elsie and I did. Work. Invest wisely. Save your money. Go against the common belief systems of others—sell when others are buying, buy when others are selling. Learn as much as you can about as much as you can. Then bless others with your knowledge and abundance."

Austin nodded, familiar with the ideas. "Avoid debt. Pay it off quickly if it happens. Share, teach, serve."

"Yes," Tommy said. "Give opportunities to people. Provide jobs for them."

Austin could practically hear Nicholas's voice in his head. He'd heard these ideas so often. "Turn to my Higher Power for knowledge and comfort. Seek inspiration by asking, listening, and acting on it."

"And most of all?" Tommy asked.

Even though Austin felt like he was back in his first lessons at the Institute, he smiled in spite of himself. "Be aware of the low frequency emotions and false narratives in my mind and body. Be willing to address and let them go. Refuse to identify with emotional baggage. It's not who I be. I can release my fears, baggage, and limiting beliefs. Ask for divine assistance and synchronicity."

Tommy nodded his approval. "Exactly. By doing these things you'll get yourself into a good position. And in doing so, you'll be in an even better position to help and bless others."

"Okay," Austin said. "I can do that."

For the first time in a long while, Austin's fears about the world beyond the Institute lessened. For all the unpredictability of modern life, he had the knowledge and tools to cope with what would be thrown at him.

"I have a final story to share with you," Tommy said.

"Okay."

"A couple once grew up in poverty in Alabama and northern Florida. They had no resources, seemingly no prospects. No money, no education. As children they had to teach themselves everything that they knew. While they came to maturity in the midst of the Great Depression, a time famous for its lack of opportunity, they managed to succeed by doing the opposite of commonly-held beliefs of the time. They'd spend the Roaring Twenties working and saving, becoming self-sufficient. This allowed them to weather the stock market crash in 1929. As other businesses floundered and sank, this couple bought up now-desperately cheap land, lumber, and mills from the cypress tree swamps of Florida. When the Second World War arrived in the 1940s, they provided cypress lumber to the US government for a war effort at a sizable premium. The couple became incredibly wealthy. This in turn helped the local economy, providing more jobs and more money to the less fortunate in their community.

"The couple triumphed because they did the opposite. They helped themselves, and then they helped others."

"That story isn't so different from yours and Elsie's," Austin said.

"No, not at all. I encourage you to ask yourself this, Austin: **what is *your* cypress crop?** Amid the turbulence and turmoil of the world, **what**

opportunities can you yourself seize to thrive in the storm? What unrealized opportunities can you find not in spite of, but because of the storm? **If you pay attention, you'll find them. Your time is here, and it's a time of amazing opportunity.** And **once you've helped yourself, you're better equipped to help others around you."**

Austin looked to the Earth below them. It held significantly less terrors for him than it did before.

"It's time for me to go back, isn't it?"

"That it is," Tommy said. "I hope you have found this information useful. May you see this time we live in with great hope and opportunity. And, one last time, as you put yourself in good places, you will in turn be able to more effectively help others."

"Thank you, Tommy. Will I ever see you again?"

"I'm sure you will." Tommy smiled. "Now, wake up."

Chapter 12 -

Austin awoke, startled out of his duality state. He had worried that everything he had learned would begin to slip through his mental fingers when he woke up, like the details of a dream, but he found his memories of his lessons with Thomas Campbell clearer than the day outside. A quick look to the alarm clock at his bedside told him that scarcely a minute had passed since Tommy carried him away in vision. Everything was exactly as he had left it, even though it seemed a lifetime ago that he first began to examine the histories and cycles of the last century.

Although his mind had wandered expanses of space and time, Austin's physical body was fresh and well-rested. He rose from the bed and set about his daily routine, beginning with consideration of his vision board.

"Austin," a voice at the door said, interrupting his rituals.

It was Taylor. She stood in the entryway, somehow aware—no doubt by way of her abilities as an Ascendant Being—that Austin had just experienced something truly remarkable.

"What are you doing here, Taylor?" Austin said. "Connor, Maleena, and your grandma are waiting for you, remember?"

"I know. I just…first I had a feeling that I needed to stay."

Austin and Taylor shared a nod of understanding. It wasn't the first time that either of them had felt strong promptings to act in one way or another. These feelings were often counterintuitive at a glance, but acting on them always proved fruitful in the end.

"I have something to tell you," Taylor said.

"Something amazing just happened," Austin began to say at the exact same moment.

The new husband and wife shared a laugh.

"You go first," Taylor said.

Austin launched into the story of all he'd experienced, his whole duality experience alongside Tommy Campbell. How it lasted longer than a lifetime, how less than a second had passed when it was over. He described the remarkable historical events to which he bore witness under Tommy's guidance. The First World War. Speakeasies and riots. Political scandals and epidemics. He explained the cycles of history to her, and how knowledge of these patterns and the turning of time's wheel. This new understanding of life helped and comforted him. Taylor nodded and listened all the while, not saying a word, and though she paid close attention to her husband's explanation, Austin sensed that her own special news held a powerful sway over her mind.

"It seems like Tommy really helped you out," Taylor said when Austin's story came to an end.

"He really did," Austin said. "I feel a lot better about the future we're going to build together. It's a little cheesy, but we'll have each other through all the hard times. And the hard times won't be nearly as frightening now that I know everything I know."

"Good," Taylor said. She smiled and kissed her husband's forehead.

"But you have something to say, too!" Austin said.

"I…I do," Taylor said. "Something amazing has happened." She hesitated, sitting down on the bed beside Austin.

"What is it? What happened?"

"Before…before I got to the car to leave with Maleena, I felt something powerful inside me. It's more like I sensed it." Taylor bit her lip, uncertain. "Austin, I know that being married to me comes with some challenges. It's not always easy being paired off with someone who became Ascendant with a bit of fruit. It's abrupt. It's different."

"Taylor," Austin said, cupping her face in his hand. "I love you. Every couple has challenges. Ours might be a little unique, but that doesn't mean we can't deal with any problem when it comes."

"No, I agree," Taylor said, leaning her being into Austin's hand and closing her eyes. "The hardest part of being your wife was knowing that I couldn't give you a child, that we couldn't start a family together. At least, not a biological one."

"I know, I know," Austin cut in, his tone gentle. "I knew that before we were married. I was perfectly happy to give that up for you."

Taylor blinked back grateful and loving tears. "I know. But something's happened. Something's changed. I can sense it inside me."

Austin pulled back to look in his wife's eyes as he started to piece it together. "What are you saying?"

"Austin," Taylor began, her voice mixed with disbelief, uncertainty, and joy. "I'm saying that I'm pregnant."

THE END

Epilogue -

Nicholas Ryan nodded to himself as he watched his mentor, Thomas Campbell, teach young Austin what wisdom he had. He felt a knot of confusion somewhere in his stomach—or at least where his stomach would be if he were observing the proceedings in physical form. He waved away the emotion for the time being, content to watch and save his questions for later.

When at last Tommy's teachings came to an end, Austin vanished from the astral space, returning to consciousness in the physical world and its illusory realities.

"You did well," Nicholas said, approaching Tommy in the weightless cosmos. "Thank you for showing Austin all of that."

Tommy nodded, not speaking, his mind elsewhere. Still with Austin.

"I do have a question for you, Master," Nicholas said. Years ago, he would have hesitated before he asked. But he felt no reservations toward his dear friend and teacher anymore. Nicholas sensed Tommy's awareness shift from Austin to him. "Why didn't you show Austin the second time strand? You only showed him the first. And why not show the me of that first time strand either?"

Both pondered their own understandings of the three time strands, all based on Taylor's key choice after eating of the fruit of immortality. The fourth strand, the one unlikely to come to pass, briefly flashed in their consciousness's as well.

"Even if I wanted to tell Austin about the other time strands, I couldn't," Tommy said, speaking at last.

Nicholas frowned, puzzled and slightly annoyed.

"Don't be too irritated with me, Master Ryan." Tommy smiled. "All three time strands are so, so close. If the Austin of this, time strand one, were to know of the other two time strands, it would definitely influence his choices going forward, and not necessarily in the best way."

"In that case," Nicholas said, "why couldn't you tell the me of that time strand about the other two?"

"For the same reason. I didn't want to unduly affect your choices. And in that strand you didn't think to look outside of linear time. Besides, you already know that you eventually learned of the other strands anyway."

Nicholas smiled ruefully. "It would have been a lot easier if I had found out earlier."

"Maybe," Tommy answered, "but it definitely would have influenced your decisions, which would have in turn influenced Austin and Taylor, too. You're too close to them, physically and emotionally, to not."

Nicholas nodded. He didn't like it, but the logic of Tommy's words was sound. He had no choice but to agree. Still, he looked to the second time strand, to that dreaded future—a future for Austin, for Taylor, and for he himself—and did nothing to combat the sorrow that weighed heavy in his heart at the thought of it. The vision danced, uncaring of his pain, behind his eyelids. Taylor's second choice. A world of hurt. The end of his own Institute. Austin's death. The literal destruction of the planet at the hands of evil in less than nine years.

It made for a painful contrast with the joyful
Austin and Taylor of the present moment, of the first
time strand. Nicholas and Tommy wordlessly
observed their joy at the unexpected but welcome
pregnancy. The happiness and new reassurance inside
Austin was tangible even with the veil between him
and the on looking masters.

"They have no idea what's coming, do they?"
Nicholas said.

"No," Tommy replied. "Not a clue. Not even
Taylor at this point in her progression."

The two men watched together in silence,
content for a moment to witness others in
contentment. Both of their hearts lay heavy with
sadness, knowing the pain that these two people they
had grown to love would soon have to experience. But
the promise of eventual triumph kept their heads held
high and their core emotions resolute and certain.

References

Ascension Training Journal –www.theascensionacademy.org

Becoming Supernatural, 2017, Dr. Joe Dispenza, Hay House, Inc., Carlsbad, CA

The Complete System of Self-Healing, 1986, Dr. Stephen T. Chang, Tao Publishing, CA

Finding your Higher Power, 2014, Audio CD, Kirk A. Duncan, 3 Key Elements, Inc.

The Future History of the United States and the World, (Coming Soon), Rex Rian

Golden Copper, 2018, Rex Rian and Camile R. Rigby

Golden Crystal, (Coming Soon), Rex Rian and Camile R. Rigby

Golden Diamond, (Coming Soon), Rex Rian and Camile R. Rigby

Golden Emerald, 2019, Rex Rian and Camile R. Rigby

Golden Sapphire, 2020, Rex Rian and Camile R. Rigby

Knowing You, 2019, Camile R. Rigby and Rex Rian

Life and Teaching of the Masters of the Far East, 1924, Baird Spalding, DeVorss Publications, CA

The Power of Awareness, 1952, Neville Goddard

Power vs. Force, 1995, Dr. David R. Hawkins, Veritas Publishing, West Sedona, AZ.

Pranic Life-Force Energy Handbook, Rex Rian and Camile R. Rigby

Zero Limits, 2007, Dr. Ihaleakala Hew Len and Dr. Joe Vitale, John Wiley & Sons

About the Author

Rex Rian is a Success Mentor, Life Coach, philosopher, and motivational speaker. As the CEO of 3 Peaks Institute of Energy and Wellness, he assists individuals and groups in their process of ascension. He finds great joy in helping others be their highest self. He lives with his wife and children in the Rocky Mountains of northern Utah.

You're welcome to contact him at www.3peaksinstitute.com or follow him on Instagram at mygoldencopper.